WALT DISNEY

POLLYANNA

Based on the novel **"***Pollyanna***"**
by Eleanor H. Porter

ADAPTED BY
ELIZABETH BEECHER

PICTURES BY
KAREN HEDSTROM

GOLDEN PRESS *New York*

THIS LITTLE GOLDEN BOOK WAS PREPARED UNDER THE SUPERVISION OF
THE WALT DISNEY STUDIO

This is the delightful story of Pollyanna, the little girl who always found something to be glad about. It was written many years ago by Eleanor H. Porter, and has long been a favorite with young and old. The story and pictures for this Little Golden Book were adapted from Walt Disney's motion picture, "Pollyanna."

Pollyanna stared around the bare little room.

"I'm glad there isn't a mirror," she said to the maid. "I won't have to look at my freckles. I'm glad, too, to have a room of my very own."

"Do you always find something to be glad about?" asked Nancy.

"I try to," said Pollyanna. "I call it playing the 'Glad Game.'"

Pollyanna was an orphan. She had just come to live with her rich Aunt Polly. Aunt Polly was very strict but she was good to Pollyanna, and bought her many lovely new clothes.

Pollyanna danced with happiness. She had never owned any brand-new clothes—only hand-me-downs.

One morning Pollyanna was walking past the orphanage when she saw a boy climbing out of a window.
He swung into a tree, and landed neatly on the
sidewalk.

"I'm Jimmy Bean," he said. "I'm an orphan."

"So am I," said Pollyanna. "My name is Pollyanna
Whittier."

"I'm going fishing," said Jimmy. "Do you want to come along?"

Pollyanna nodded, and away they went to the stream. They had no hook. Instead they used a tin can tied to a string. They did not catch a single fish—but they had fun.

On the way home, Jimmy took Pollyanna into a big, overgrown garden. "Here is the tallest tree in town," he said. "Be very quiet. Old Man Pendergast lives here, and he hates kids."

Pollyanna was a little scared but she followed Jimmy
to the tree.

"I'm going to climb the tree," said Jimmy. "I bet
I can see the whole town from the top."

He started to shinny up the trunk when—crash!—a
wild-eyed old man burst out of the underbrush.

"Jiggers!" yelled Jimmy. "It's Pendergast!"

Pendergast grabbed for Pollyanna, but she ducked out of his reach. Jimmy was not as lucky. Pendergast seized him and dragged him into the house.

"Help!" screamed Jimmy.

Pollyanna wanted to run away. But Jimmy was her friend. She must try to help him.

Bravely, she headed into the house. Pendergast and Jimmy were in the living room. The old man was trying to telephone the police.

"You let Jimmy go!" Pollyanna said loudly. "He didn't hurt anything, and neither did I."

Pendergast was so surprised that he let go of the boy. Jimmy dashed for the door, and disappeared quickly, before the old man could catch him.

Pendergast glared at Pollyanna. "Go on—get out of here!" he bellowed.

Pollyanna started out, then stopped short. On the wall were beautiful patches of colored light.

"What a beautiful rainbow!" she gasped.

"That's not a rainbow," scowled Pendergast. "It's the sun shining through the prisms of the lamp."

"I like to think it's a rainbow," said Pollyanna.

"Bosh!" snorted Pendergast.

Pollyanna laughed. "Maybe you're not glad I came here, but I am," she said as she skipped merrily out of the room.

A few days later, Pollyanna and Nancy brought baskets of food to some of the poor families in town. The last basket was for old Mrs. Snow.

Mrs. Snow was a cranky old lady. She found fault with everything and everybody—even Pollyanna.

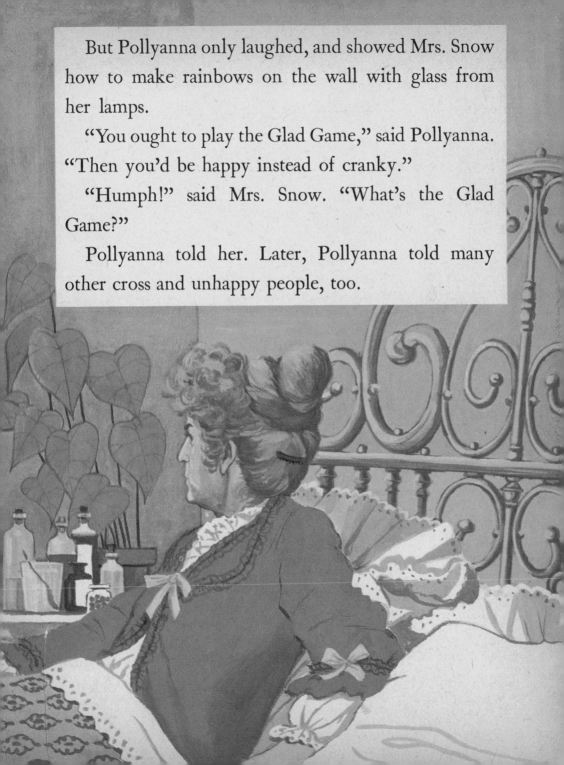

But Pollyanna only laughed, and showed Mrs. Snow how to make rainbows on the wall with glass from her lamps.

"You ought to play the Glad Game," said Pollyanna. "Then you'd be happy instead of cranky."

"Humph!" said Mrs. Snow. "What's the Glad Game?"

Pollyanna told her. Later, Pollyanna told many other cross and unhappy people, too.

One day the people of the town decided to hold a big fair. They wanted to raise money to build a new orphanage. The old one was almost ready to fall down.

Pollyanna was excited about the fair, and did all she could to help. She even asked Old Man Pendergast to take a booth and sell glass pendants.

"We'll call them rainbow-makers," said Pollyanna. And Mrs. Snow promised to make a quilt.

Doctor Chilton told Aunt Polly about the fair.

"We don't need a new orphanage," she scowled. "I'll pay for repairs on the old one."

"The people do not want your charity," said Doctor Chilton. "They want to raise the money themselves."

This made Aunt Polly very angry. "You stay away from that fair," she told Pollyanna.

"But they're going to have a parade with lighted lanterns," said Pollyanna, "and free corn-on-the-cob, and ice cream and—"

"Be quiet!" snapped Aunt Polly. "You're not going and that's the end of it!"

But Pollyanna did go.

Jimmy Bean helped her climb down the big tree outside her attic window. They were so quiet, Aunt Polly did not hear them.

At the fair, Pollyanna and Jimmy ate ice cream, and watermelon, and taffy apples, and corn-on-the-cob.

And Pollyanna pulled a beautiful big doll out of the fish-pond booth.

"Oooh!" she cried. "Am I glad! I never had a doll of my own before!"

When Pollyanna got home, she climbed up the tree easily. But as she jumped over to the windowsill, she slipped and fell to the ground.

Aunt Polly heard Pollyanna scream, and hurried outside. Pollyanna was lying very, very still.

"She is badly hurt," Aunt Polly told Nancy. "Call Doctor Chilton! And hurry!"

The next day, Doctor Chilton told Pollyanna that
her legs were hurt, and that she must go to the hospital.

"I won't go," said Pollyanna. "I'll never get well.
And I'll never be glad again in my whole life, either."

Aunt Polly was sad when she heard this. She really
loved Pollyanna very much.

So did everyone in town. That afternoon, they all came to see her. They brought her gifts, and lots and lots of love.

Jimmy and Pendergast came, too. "Mr. Pendergast's adopted me," said Jimmy.

"Oh, I'm so glad!" cried Pollyanna before she thought. Then she smiled at Aunt Polly. "I will go to the hospital, Aunt Polly—and I'll get well for you and all my friends."

And she did!